HOW TO BE A CAT

Nikki McClure

Abrams Appleseed
New York

STRETCH

CLEAN

POUNCE

BRAVE

HUNT

LICK

STALK

CHASE

WAIT

FIND

SCRATCH

FEAST

DREAM

TO MENTORS, ESPECIALLY GEORGIA MUNGER.

How to Be a Cat was inspired by Bud, the cat who came with the house I bought in 2001. "Don't worry, the neighbors feed him. He just sleeps in the garage." I was told. But Bud, blind and old, took to me. He would climb on my back while I gardened. Eventually, it was I who fed him and he became family. I made a calendar featuring Bud in 2001. It chronicled my adventures as I made my new house a home. For this book, I revisited the calendar artwork and made all new images, adding a kitten. Bud remains old and blind, and endlessly patient ... almost.

The artwork was cut from black paper. Color was added digitally.

Cataloging-in-Publication Data has been applied for and may be obtained from the Library of Congress.

ISBN: 978-1-4197-0528-1

Text and illustrations copyright © 2013 Nikki McClure

Book design by Chad W. Beckerman

Printed and bound in U.S.A.
10 9 8 7 6 5 4 3 2 1

For bulk discount inquiries, contact specialsales@abramsbooks.com.

ABRAMS
THE ART OF BOOKS SINCE 1949

115 West 18th Street
New York, NY 10011
www.abramsbooks.com